Great-Granny Rose
and the
Family Christmas Tree

Great-Granny Rose and the Family Christmas Tree

Ann Edwards Cannon

Illustrated by Jacqui Grothe

DESERET BOOK COMPANY
SALT LAKE CITY, UTAH

For my grandmother Louise Covey, in loving memory—A.E.C.

For Nana Toddy and all grandmothers who take time to share stories—J.G.

Text copyright © 1996 Ann Edwards Cannon
Illustrations copyright © 1996 Jacqui Grothe

Library of Congress Cataloging-in-Publication Data
Cannon, A. E. (Ann Edwards)
Great-Granny Rose and the family Christmas tree /
Ann Edwards Cannon : illustrated by Jacqui Grothe.
p.   cm.
Summary: Great-Granny Rose and four-year-old Joey bring her
new Christmas tree to life by decorating it with a box of old ornaments,
each of which has its own story or association.

ISBN 1-57345-118-5

[1. Christmas trees—Fiction. 2. Christmas—Fiction. 3. Great-grandmothers—Fiction.]
I. Grothe, Jacqui, 1962–   ill.   II. Title.
PZ7.C17135Gr   1996
[E]—dc20   96-8466
CIP   AC

Printed in Mexico
10 9 8 7 6 5 4 3 2 1

This book belongs to

The Gammell's 2002 ~~2003~~ oops.

Merry Christmas!

The Butterfield's

Great-Granny Rose was so old her hair was white as snow and her face was seamed with wrinkles.

When Joey, who was four, asked her how old she was, she only smiled and said, "Older than the trees in my front yard."

Great-Granny Rose's things were old, too. The wedding ring on her finger was worn thin. The couch by the window where she sat to catch the sun on her shoulders was faded. The Bible she kept on the low table had pages as brittle dry as last year's leaves.

Even Great-Granny Rose's cat, Moses, was old. He didn't bother with chasing mice anymore but preferred sitting next to Great-Granny Rose and flicking his tangerine tail.

Joey liked Moses and Great-Granny Rose's house and Great-Granny Rose, too.

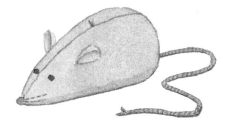

One Saturday in December, Joey and Dad took Great-Granny Rose a Christmas tree and set it in a sturdy stand near the window, not far from the couch.

"How do you like your Christmas tree?" Dad asked in a loud voice as he filled the stand with water.

Great-Granny Rose looked at it with her cloudy blue eyes and blinked. But she didn't answer.

Dad went to the hall closet and pulled down a big brown box from the top shelf. He placed it by the tree. Joey wondered what was inside.

"We'll help you decorate later," said Dad, "but I have some errands to run right now."

"It isn't alive," Great-Granny Rose finally said.

"Excuse me?" Dad looked confused.

"The tree," said Great-Granny Rose. "It isn't alive."

"Oh, but it is," Dad answered. "Smell it, Great-Granny Rose. That's fresh Christmas tree smell, all right."

Then he walked to the couch and dropped a kiss on Great-Granny Rose's snow-white head. "Good-bye for now."

Joey really wanted to see what was in the box. "Can I stay?" he asked. "Please?"

"Please?" Great-Granny Rose echoed.

Dad looked at them both and then looked at his watch. "Fine. I'll be back in an hour."

As soon as the door shut, Joey raced over to the big brown box and removed the lid. Inside were Christmas tree ornaments, dozens and dozens of them, shining and still as pirates' treasure.

Carefully, Joey lifted an ornament and looked at it. The clouds in Great-Granny Rose's eyes parted.

"Now *that* was my mother's. She hung it on her own tree when she was a young married woman in England. She and my father lived in a lovely little cottage in Bristol with china and fine furniture. But when they heard the missionaries, they decided to come to America, where I was born. They sold many of their possessions, although not quite everything."

Joey took that ornament from long ago and hung it on the tree.

Then he lifted another from the box.

"Now *that* was on my tree when I was a girl," said Great-Granny Rose. "On Christmas Day my brothers and I hitched up the horses for a great sleigh ride. Then we went skating on the lake with friends. After, we all drank hot cider."

Joey took that ornament from long ago and hung it on the tree. Then he lifted another from the box.

"Now *that* was your grandmother's favorite ornament when she was a little girl," said Great-Granny Rose. "Times were terribly hard then. It was the Great Depression, and strong men couldn't find work. We were lucky. My husband had a job with the railroad."

Joey took that ornament from long ago and hung it on the tree. Then he lifted another from the box.

"Now *that* was an ornament your father loved to play with," said Great-Granny Rose. "I remember the year he found a cowboy hat and holster with two cap guns waiting for him beneath the Christmas tree. He looked just like you look now."

Joey took that ornament from long ago and hung it on the tree. Then he lifted another from the box—his favorite. No doubt about it.

"Now *that* was an ornament some special young man made for me with his own two hands," said Great-Granny Rose. "Who would that be?"

"That would be me," said Joey.

He took that ornament from not so long ago and hung it on the tree. Then he hung more and more until the box was empty and the tree was full.

Slowly, very slowly, Great-Granny Rose stood up and joined Joey. She slipped one old hand over his. Together they stood and looked at the green branches bobbing and brimming with glass balls and bells, beads and painted birds.

"And now," announced Great-Granny Rose, "my tree is alive!"